Now I'm stuck living in the middle of nowhere with Mom, her stupid husband, and his disgusting son Ronald.

When we first got to our new house, Walter and Ronald were waiting for us. Walter tried to kiss me hello, but I pushed him away. Ronald didn't say a word. He just stood there staring down at his feet.

After a few minutes, Walter took us all upstairs. I looked at my new room. It was much bigger than my room in Brooklyn. Ronald's room was right across the hall from mine. He had a big sign on his door that said "Ronald's Room. Keep Out."

"Listen, dog face," Ronald said to me as I read the sign. "If I catch you in my room, you're dead meat."

"I'd sooner die than touch any of your junk," I said. "And speaking of rooms, make sure you stay out of mine."

"I see the kids are starting off on the right foot," Mom said to Walter.

"Don't worry, Susan. We can handle it," Walter said.

Right!

Does Third Grade Last Forever?

Mindy Schanback

Cover by Susan Tang
Illustrated by Paul Henry

Troll Associates

Library of Congress Cataloging-in-Publication Data

Schanback, Mindy.
    Does third grade last forever? / by Mindy Schanback; illustrated
by Paul Henry.
        p.   cm.—(Making the grade)
    Summary: When her mother remarries, eight-year-old Tracy has to
get used to a new school and a new obnoxious stepbrother.
    ISBN 0-8167-1700-1 (lib. bdg.)   ISBN 0-8167-1701-X (pbk.)
    [1. Remarriage—Fiction.   2. Stepchildren—Fiction.   3. Schools—
Fiction.]   I. Henry, Paul, 1956-   ill. II. Title. III. Series:
Making the grade (Mahwah, N.J.)
PZ7.S33375Do   1990
[Fic]—dc20   89-20603

A TROLL BOOK, published by Troll Associates.

Does Third Grade Last Forever?

To Jeffrey, with love and devotion

◆ Chapter 1 ◆

*M*others! They promise you they'll never get married again, and next thing you know you're a bridesmaid.

Mom said that during a wedding a bridesmaid had to act very grown-up. That meant that you couldn't run away screaming when your new stepfather asked you to dance. Even if you wanted to.

Just so you know, my name is Tracy. Tracy Crane. I was living in Park Slope. That's in Brooklyn, New York.

Walter Stacy was going to be my new stepfather. He was fat and ugly and I hated him.

"May I have this dance please?" Walter asked me. He smiled and held out his hand. I swallowed and smiled bravely.

"That would be very nice," I lied. Walter took my arm and led me to the dance floor.

Besides being fat and ugly, Walter was an awful dancer. I looked across the dance floor. Mom was dancing with Ronald. He was my new stepbrother, and I hated him even more than I hated Walter.

"You've got to give Ronald a chance," Mom had told me as we were getting dressed for the wedding.

"Easy for you to say," I mumbled back as I slipped my bridesmaid dress over my head. "Ronald doesn't call you 'dog face.'"

Walter whirled me around the dance floor. "Are you enjoying the wedding?" he asked.

Enjoy? He had to be kidding. That was the worst day of my life. "Ow," I squealed as Walter stepped on my foot for the third time.

"Sorry," he said.

I started to think about how bad my mom was going to feel when I needed foot surgery. She'd sit by my hospital bed and beg me to forgive her. But I wouldn't. Not ever.

I couldn't believe it when Mom told me the news. We were grocery-shopping in our neighborhood supermarket. Mom put some cereal into our shopping cart, then said, "I've got news, Tracy."

"Did you get me the new bicycle I wanted?" I asked. I'd been hoping for a new bike for a long time. A red one, with a real wicker basket and a little bell.

"No," Mom said. "Nothing like that." She took a deep breath, then looked me in the eye. "I've decided to get married."

"What!" I screamed at the top of my lungs. I yelled so loud that the two old ladies down the aisle turned around to stare at me.

"Tracy! Could you please keep it down?" Mom asked as she kept wheeling the grocery cart.

I followed her over to the fruit section. "Married!" I said a little softer this time. "To who?"

"To *whom*, Tracy."

"Mother!"

"To a very nice man named Walter Stacy," Mom answered. She looked over the fruit. "Do you want some bananas?"

This was no time to talk about bananas. "You can't get married," I said. "What about Dad?"

"We've been divorced for six years," Mom said. She threw a bunch of bananas into the cart.

"I know *that*."

"Don't be fresh, Tracy." Mom moved briskly toward the checkout line. Then she dropped another bombshell.

"Walter has a really nice nine-year-old son named Ronald." This time she didn't even bother to look at me.

I couldn't believe this was happening. "No, no, no," I moaned.

"I know this is very hard for you, Tracy," Mom said. "But you'll see. Once you've settled in, you'll love Greatdale."

"Greatdale? Long Island? You mean you're moving?"

"*We're* moving, Tracy," Mom said calmly. "You and I." She began unloading the cart.

Mom and I didn't really say anything else to each other until we got home. I was too upset to speak. I couldn't even look at her.

That night, while we were watching TV, Mom told me how much I'd like living in Greatdale, what fun I'd have in a big house, how I'd get to go to a new school and how much I'd enjoy having a big brother.

I was sure I would hate it. When she finished talking, I stood up and looked her right in the eye. "Mom," I said, "you cannot get married." Then I turned and left the room.

That was two weeks before. So there I was at her wedding, dancing with my new stepfather. And if he stepped on my foot one more time, I was going to kick him.

My folks got divorced when I was two. Since then I've lived with my mom, except that I always spend the summer in Maine with my dad.

For the past three summers, Mom had

worked at the Greatdale Inn. She's a chef, and a good one, too. Mom said you had to be good to work at the Greatdale Inn.

The Inn is real famous, and lots of rich people go there. Walter owns the Inn. He was divorced, too, so I guess with that, and working together for so long, he and Mom had a lot in common. Even so, it was hard for me to believe Mom fell in love with him. He's fat, he hardly has any hair, and he makes the stupidest conversation.

"Hello, Tracy," he said when we first met. "You're as pretty as your mother said you were."

"Then she must have said I'm a real dog," I answered. That shut him up.

Actually, I'm not bad looking. I may not be a beauty, but I've got nice, straight dark brown hair and big brown eyes. I'm even tall for my age.

Mom and Walter decided not to take a honeymoon after their wedding. So the day after the wedding, Mom and I moved to Greatdale.

When we got there, Walter and Ronald were waiting for us. Walter tried to kiss me hello, but I pushed him away. Ronald didn't say a word. He just stood there staring down at his feet.

After a few minutes, Walter took us all upstairs. I looked at my new room. It was much bigger than my room in Brooklyn. Ronald's room was right across the hall from mine. He had a big sign on his door. It said, "Ronald's Room. Keep Out."

"Yo, dog face," Ronald said to me as I read the sign. "I mean it. If I catch you in my room, you're dead meat."

"I'd sooner die than touch any of your junk," I said. "And, speaking of rooms, make sure you stay out of mine."

"I see the kids are starting off on the right foot," Mom said to Walter.

"Don't worry, Susan. We can handle it," Walter said. Right!

After I unpacked my stuff, Walter showed me around Greatdale. It's tiny, and not at all like Brooklyn. The streets and sidewalks are really wide, and I don't think I saw one bus.

Mom and Walter took Ronald and me to the Greatdale Inn. I hated to admit it, but it was beautiful. It was so pretty, in fact, that I forgot that I didn't want to talk to Walter.

"Wow, this place is super," I said.

He looked so pleased that for a minute I almost liked him. Then he introduced me to the people who worked there as his new little stepdaughter. It was gross. They all said dumb things, too, like, "My, what a big girl you are," or "How did you get so many freckles?"

How would they like it if I said to them,

"My, what a fat woman you are," or "How did you get so many wrinkles?"

After looking around town, we went to the sweet shop for a snack. "I'll have a chocolate soda," I told the lady behind the counter.

Walter talked to my mom the whole time we were eating. He talked about the town and what our life would be like as a family. How glad he was that Mom and I were going to be living with him and Ronald.

I didn't say anything. After a while he stopped speaking and took a bite out of his sundae. "Why don't you talk for a while?" he said.

"I don't have anything to say." I took one last, noisy sip of my soda.

When we got home, I went into my room and closed the door. My favorite doll Nellie was sitting on my bed. I don't know why, but suddenly I was crying. I hugged Nellie and cried for a long time.

Chapter 2

Walter's house is big. It's two stories tall, and there are five bedrooms on the second floor.

Mom loved it. Why, I don't know. The roof leaks, the furniture sags, and if you run the dishwasher or the washing machine, you can't take a hot bath for about an hour.

The outside is white except for the trim, which is dark green. The backyard is huge. It has two gardens: a big one near the house for flowers, and a little one at the far end for vegetables.

It's amazing how many vegetables you can get from a small garden, especially tomatoes. After the first week, we'd had tomato soup, tomato sauce, tomato salad, pickled tomatoes, stewed tomatoes, fried tomatoes, and tomatoes with cream.

"If I ever have another tomato, it'll be too soon," I said. Mom smiled. She was making tomato omelets.

Mom had been smiling a lot the last couple of days. She and Walter would go around calling each other "honey" and "darling" every five minutes. It was gross.

Luckily, I only had one more day around the house. It was Labor Day, so school was starting the next week. Mom was planning a holiday barbecue and she even invited Walter's mother. Mom said I had to call Walter's mother Grandma Connie. I wanted to tell her to forget it, but I didn't want to hurt her feelings.

I only met Grandma Connie once since the wedding. She came to help us move in, but wasn't much help. All she did was eat and order everybody around.

"Put those pots in there, Susan," she said, pointing to the cabinets.

"I always hang my pots on a wall," Mom said firmly. Mom's very fussy about her kitchen.

"Well, don't complain to me when they fall down," Grandma Connie answered. She took a bite out of a brownie. "These brownies aren't sweet enough. Where did you get them?"

"I made them."

"They'd be better if you added more sugar," Grandma Connie said. She took another bite.

"It hasn't stopped you from eating three of them," I heard Mom mutter under her breath.

By the time we got to the living room, Mom was tired of arguing. She let Grandma Connie decide where to put our lamps, stacking tables, and little knickknacks.

"See," Grandma Connie said to Mom when we were finished, "lots of hands make light work."

"Too many cooks spoil the broth," Mom mumbled.

"What?" said Grandma Connie.

"Nothing," Mom said sweetly. "You must be tired after all your hard work."

"I am, rather," Grandma Connie said, sitting down with a thump.

"Me, too," I said, flopping down beside her. "Are there any more brownies?"

After eating some more brownies, Grandma Connie left. As soon as she walked out the door, Mom started to rearrange the room.

"Come on, Tracy, give me a hand with this chair," Mom said. She gave it a push.

I went over to help her. "How come you told Grandma Connie you liked the way she set up the room if you didn't?" I asked.

"I didn't want to hurt her feelings," Mom

said, giving me a big grin. "And you know the old saying, 'what they don't know won't hurt them.' "

On the day of the barbecue, the weather was warm and sunny. "It's a perfect day for a barbecue, isn't it, darling?" Walter said, sitting down at the breakfast table.

"Just lovely, sweetheart," Mom agreed. "I know we're all going to have a terrific time."

Ronald rolled his eyes. I could tell he didn't think so.

After breakfast, I got stuck with the dishes. I was just putting away the silverware when I saw Ronald and Walter through the kitchen window. They were in the backyard, and it looked like they were arguing. I opened the window so I could hear.

"I'm sorry you feel that way, Ronald, but you can't go out today," Walter said firmly. "You have to stay home and help Susan, Tracy and me make a nice family barbecue."

Ronald scowled up at him. "I hate Susan and Tracy!" he yelled.

"Calm down, Ronald," Walter said, putting his hand on Ronald's shoulder.

Ronald shrugged Walter off and kicked at a rock.

"Why don't you tell me why you don't like Susan and Tracy?"

They were just getting to the good stuff when Mom called me. "Tracy, I need you to help me," she called from the living room.

"One minute."

"Now, Tracy," Mom said. I could tell from her voice that she meant business.

I took one last look out the window. Ronald was walking around the side of the house. He didn't look very happy. His shoulders were slumped and he had a big frown on his face.

The barbecue was scheduled for five. At three-thirty, Grandma Connie showed up. Mom answered the door. She was still wearing her bathrobe and her hair was wet.

When Grandma Connie saw Mom, she shook her head. "Tsk, tsk, tsk," she said, frowning. "Still in your bathrobe, I see."

"I just got out of the shower," Mom said. She ran her fingers through her damp hair and tried to smile.

Grandma Connie came in and said hello to me. Then she handed Mom a brown paper bag filled with tomatoes. "A little something from my garden."

I looked in the bag, then started to giggle. "That makes about a million tomatoes," I said.

Mom glared at me. "The correct thing to say is 'thank you,'" she said sharply.

"But Mom, you said yourself that we were drowning in tomatoes."

"Well, if you don't want them, just say so," Grandma Connie sniffed.

"No, no, you can't have too many tomatoes," Mom said cheerfully. "Run and put these with the others, will you, Tracy."

Grandma Connie went into the living room. "I see you've rearranged the furniture," she said.

I walked into the kitchen. The windowsill was covered with tomatoes. I tried to make room for the ones Grandma Connie brought, but there was no way they were going to fit. Then I got a brilliant idea. I went over to the trash and dumped Grandma Connie's tomatoes in.

"What they don't know won't hurt them," I whispered to myself.

I looked out the window. Walter and Ronald were putting charcoal into the grill.

Mom came into the kitchen. "I want to get dressed. Can you do me a favor? Talk to Grandma Connie. She's in the living room."

"All right," I said with a sigh.

"That's a good girl," Mom said. She gave me a quick hug.

I went to find Grandma Connie. She was bending down behind the couch. She looked up and saw me watching her. "Can you help me plug this in, Tracy? I can't get to the outlet."

"It was plugged in," I said. I knew because I had been reading next to it the night before.

"I think it looks better over here," Grandma Connie said. I helped her plug in the lamp, then went upstairs to find Mom.

She was standing at the dresser putting on her makeup. "Mom," I said, "Grandma Connie is rearranging the living room again."

"Oh, no," Mom said. "Try to distract her. I'll be right down."

For dinner we were having tomato-and-onion salad, barbecued chicken, hamburgers, hot dogs, grilled tomatoes and potato skins. Dessert was ice cream and cake.

I was in the kitchen making hamburger patties when Walter came in. "I appreciate your helping us," Walter said.

"I'm helping my mother."

Walter looked uncomfortable. "I know this is hard for you. I just want to say that I hope we'll be friends. I'm not trying to replace your father."

I felt tears come to my eyes. "You're not my father, and there's no way you could replace him."

I ran outside. How could he say something so stupid? He had to be the dumbest man in the world. I ran smack into my mother and Ronald.

"I'm not looking to replace your mother. I just want us to be friends," Mom was saying.

The afternoon dragged on. Finally dinner was ready. Mom got everyone seated around the outdoor table and began serving the food. Ronald ate a hamburger, two hot dogs, a dozen potato skins, a piece of chicken and a slice of cake.

"You shouldn't let him eat any more," said Grandma Connie. "Ronald has a very sensitive stomach."

Mom tried to smile, but I could tell she was getting annoyed. That was about the fifth time Grandma Connie had told her what to do. "Oh, he'll stop when he's full," Mom said.

About a minute later Ronald got sick. He ran a couple of feet and then threw up in the tomato patch. *So much for our tomato problem,* I thought. I held my hand to my mouth and tried not to laugh.

When Ronald got back to the table, my mother asked if he was feeling better. "You really turned green," I said, giggling.

"Think you're funny, don't you, dog breath?" Ronald said. Then he dumped the cake I was eating right into my lap.

I leaped up from the table and went to hit him, but Ronald was too fast for me. He jumped on his bicycle and rode off.

"You should discipline the children," Grandma Connie said to Mom.

Walter came out of the house carrying five plates of ice cream. "Everyone having a good time?" he asked cheerfully.

Finally, the party was over. Mom went into the living room and fell over some stacking tables. Grandma Connie must have moved them.

"Great party, Mom," I said.

She laughed. "Thanks, Tracy. Remind me to give another one, say New Year's Eve, 2749."

◆ Chapter 3 ◆

I never thought I'd say this, but I was glad the day school started. I was getting tired of hanging around the house, listening to my mom and Walter call each other "honey" all the time.

Walter wanted me to use his last name, but Tracy Stacy ... yuck. It's scary enough starting a new school without having a name you know everyone's going to make fun of. Anyway, Crane is my dad's name, and I wanted to keep it. I told my mother I'd always been Tracy Crane and I always will be.

Mom didn't even have to wake me up that morning. I was up and dressed by six-thirty.

I was too worried about school to eat anything at breakfast. "Eat your eggs, Tracy," Mom said.

I tried, but I just couldn't swallow. "How am I going to get to school?" I asked.

"Ronald will take you," Walter said.

"Dad! I can't go walking to school with a girl," said Ronald. "Besides, I always ride my bike with Elliot." Elliot is Ronald's best friend.

Mom smiled. "Show her, Walter," she said.

"Look outside, Tracy," said Walter.

I ran to the front door. On the porch was a really neat red bicycle with a wicker basket and a little bell. "Wow! Thanks, Mom!" I said, hugging her.

"Thank Walter," Mom said. "It was his idea."

"Thank you, Walter," I said politely. I held out my hand and he shook it.

"Now, let Tracy ride with you," Walter said to Ronald, giving him a stern look. "And no funny business."

Elliot rode up on his bike. "You and Ronald will be showing Tracy the way to school," Walter said to him. "If you do a good job, I'll take you to the movies."

"Popcorn, too?" Elliot asked.

"Popcorn, too," Walter said, smiling.

"All right," Elliot said, jumping up and down. I sort of liked Elliot at that moment. He was really tall and skinny and a lot nicer than

Ronald. I know that wasn't saying much, though.

"Ronald?" Walter asked.

Ronald kicked the porch floor and scowled. "All right," he sighed. "If it's okay with Elliot I guess I can stand it."

"Good boy," Walter said, patting him on the back. I hopped on my bike.

"Let's go," I said.

Ronald got on his bike, and the three of us rode off down the street.

"Not too fast," Mom called after us. When we rounded the corner, Ronald yelled, "Catch us if you can." Then he and Elliot rode as fast as they could.

"Slow down," I yelled behind them. I pedaled hard, but could barely keep up. By the time we got to school, I was breathing so hard I could hardly talk.

"I'm going to tell my mother," I panted. We parked our bikes.

"Tattletale," Ronald said. He stuck his tongue out at me. Then he and Elliot ran off for the fourth-grade line. So much for liking Elliot.

Mom told me to go right to the principal's office. I had to register and find out whose class I'd be in. Mrs. Fulsom is the principal at Southside. She's all wrinkled up, and looks like she's about 110.

"Hello, Tracy Crane," she said in a quivery

voice. "Welcome to Southside Elementary School."

She told me that Ms. Maxwell was going to be my third-grade teacher. As we walked down the hall to Ms. Maxwell's class, my stomach started to hurt. What if Ms. Maxwell didn't like me? What if no one talked to me? What if everyone made fun of me?

By the time I got to class I felt so sick I almost asked Mrs. Fulsom to call my mother. The class was saying the "Pledge of Allegiance."

" . . . one nation, under God, indivisible, with liberty and justice for all."

I held my hand over my heart like everyone else while I tried to keep up with the words. But I wasn't paying attention. I was too scared.

The first thing Ms. Maxwell did was a seating chart. I was in the middle of the fifth row. I sat down in between a girl named Leslie and a boy with brown hair named Mike. The girl across from me was named Sharon. She had bright red hair, and she gave me a big smile when I sat down.

Ms. Maxwell looked like she was going to be okay. She didn't yell at anyone, not even at this big guy Micky when he threw a paper airplane.

She expected a lot from us, though. "This year we're going to learn the multiplication tables through twelve, how to write in script, and all about the continents and solar system."

Except for multiplication, it didn't sound too bad. I already knew a lot about the planets because Dad had a telescope. When you looked into it, you could see the craters on the moon.

The rest of the morning was easy. We went around the room and introduced ourselves. I just talked about me and Mom. I didn't say a word about Walter or Ronald because I didn't think it was anybody's business.

Then Ms. Maxwell handed out our textbooks and told us the class rules. Right before lunch we had our first real class of the day— math.

"The first two chapters in your textbooks go over what you learned last year," Ms. Maxwell said, "and we're going to start out with that."

I flipped through the textbook. The kids at Southside already learned how to subtract three- and four-digit numbers from each other. We hadn't done that yet in my old school. I started to get worried again.

Luckily, Ms. Maxwell stuck to simple addition for the first day. Even so, math seemed to go on forever. Finally the lunch bell rang.

"Line up, everybody," Ms. Maxwell said. She marched us into the school cafeteria. Mom had made my favorite, a BLT with mayonnaise on white bread. At the bottom of the bag was a little note. "Dear Tracy, here's hoping your first day is great."

I felt tears come to my eyes, but I stopped myself from crying. All I had to do was start crying in the middle of the school cafeteria, and I'd never make any friends. A bunch of kids from my class were eating together, but I was too shy to go over and talk to them.

Instead, I looked at the math textbook I had with me. There's nothing more boring than a math book, but I tried to look at it like it was a big thrill.

After lunch we had reading, social studies, then finally gym. Our gym teacher was named Mr. Boggs, and he was fat, which is funny for a P.E. teacher.

"Balls and rackets over here, kids," Mr. Boggs said. We were outside in a big field behind the school. Right next to the field were six tennis courts. Mr. Boggs had us play tennis in teams of four. I was playing with Leslie and Mike, the kids in my row, and some kid named Andrew.

"Whammo," yelled Andrew. He hit the ball to me so hard that his glasses fell off. I missed.

"Sorry," I said. My partner Mike grinned at me. When he smiled I saw that he had a big space between his two front teeth.

"Don't worry about it," Mike said. He hit

the ball cross court to Leslie. She hit it back to me. I missed.

"Sorry," I said again. Dad taught me to play tennis, so I'm usually a pretty good player. Not that day though. I must have said sorry about fifteen times.

"I hate gym," Leslie said as we were handing back our rackets. I smiled at her but couldn't think of anything to say. Then, on the way back to class, I heard her say to Andrew, "That new girl is stuck-up."

I was so upset that I didn't even hear Andrew's answer. Stuck-up? Me? I was just shy, that's all.

When I got home, Mom asked me how school went.

"Okay," I answered.

"And the other kids?"

My voice cracked. "Okay." I could feel a tear drip down my cheek.

"Oh, honey, are you crying?" Mom said. She came over to hug me, but I ducked and ran up the stairs.

"Stop asking me questions," I yelled. "And, no—I'm not crying."

I decided to call Dad. He never asked me stupid questions. He just listened.

Dad picked up the phone on the first ring. "Hi, Daddy, I miss you so much," I blurted out.

"I miss you, too, honey," he said. I knew he meant it. Dad and I always had great times together. We both liked playing sports and going to science museums.

"I started school today," I said. "We're going to learn about the solar system, but the kids already know how to subtract big numbers from each other."

"Well, that sounds fair. You probably know a lot more than the other kids about the planets, and they know more about subtraction than you do."

"But math is my worst subject," I said, gulping back more tears.

"Don't worry. I'll help you, and if that doesn't work, I'll talk to your mom about hiring a tutor."

I paused for a minute. "Daddy, do you think I'm stuck-up?" I asked in a tiny voice.

"I think you're delightful."

Fathers are so great.

Chapter 4

*O*ur first class project was a booklet on the continents for social studies. There are seven continents: Europe, Asia, Africa, North America, South America, Australia, and Antarctica.

Using stencils Ms. Maxwell gave us, we drew each of the continents on a different page and labeled the oceans around them. I used a different color pencil for each of my continents, and did little waves in my oceans.

I wanted my first project to be really good. Dad told me that once your teacher gets an idea of what kind of student you are, she sticks to it. I wanted Ms. Maxwell to stick to the idea that I got good grades.

I was beginning to get to know the other

kids in my class. Leslie sat in front of me. She had blond hair and blue eyes, and she was the prettiest girl in the class. She also wore the nicest clothes. She talked a lot to Sharon, but never turned around to talk to me.

She thought I was stuck-up. Well, I thought she was. If I was sitting in front of someone, I'd turn around to talk. Mike sat behind me, and I talked to him all the time. He was nice, but a little shy.

I liked Sharon the best. She was always getting into trouble, but she was funny. When she got caught passing a note to Leslie, she said that she was practicing her script.

Even Ms. Maxwell had to laugh. It was hard for a teacher to stay mad at Sharon because she got the best grades in class. So far she'd gotten a hundred on every homework assignment.

Ms. Maxwell never really got mad at anyone. Not even at Micky. Micky was the biggest guy in the class and dumb. He never knew the answer to any of the questions Ms. Maxwell asked, even the easy ones. He also picked fights. I tried to stay away from him.

Math was the first subject of the day, and every day Ms. Maxwell started the class with a contest. Everyone had to stand up while she went around the room asking addition problems.

"Six plus two, Leslie."

"Eight."

"That's right. Three plus four, Tracy."

"Seven."

"Good."

If you missed the question, then you had to sit down and do extra addition problems.

Every day there were five people left standing. They won and didn't have to do any extra work.

Things were going pretty well until Ms. Maxwell gave away my secret, right in front of the whole class. She was taking attendance.

"Tracy Crane."

I raised my hand. "Here," I said.

"One of the teachers told me that Walter Stacy is your stepfather," Ms. Maxwell said.

I was so nervous I knocked over my pencil box. Different-colored pencils spilled all over the floor. "That's right," I said.

"How come you never mentioned it?" she asked.

I bent over to pick up my pencils. "I forgot," I mumbled.

Ms. Maxwell looked at me funny. I could tell she didn't believe me. After all it's hard to forget your stepfamily.

"I know your stepbrother," Sharon told me later on at lunch. She sat down next to me and took out her sandwich. "He's friends with my brother Bill."

"I hate him," I said. I unwrapped my sandwich. It was peanut butter and jelly.

"Yuck," I said, making a face. "I hate peanut butter and jelly."

"I love it," Sharon said. "I have chicken. Want to trade?"

"Deal," I said. We traded sandwiches.

"How come you hate Ronald?" Sharon asked.

"Because he's always picking on me," I said.

She nodded. "He teases me, too." She tossed her red hair. "But I don't let it bother me."

We ate quietly for a minute. Then she said, "I live in a stepfamily, too."

"You do?" I was so surprised that I stopped eating and stared at Sharon.

"Yeah. I live with my mother and stepfather, my big brother Bill and my half-sister Debbie. Then, every other weekend, my stepbrother Bruce comes to stay with us. Every couple of months, Bill and I go to see my Dad. He lives in Minnesota."

"Wow. And I thought I had it bad," I said.

Sharon took the last bite of her sandwich. "My stepdad doesn't care about Bill and me at all," she said. "Sometimes I'm sure he'd like to get rid of us, but my mother won't let him. I bet your stepdad wants to get rid of you, too."

I thought about it. What if Walter really did want to get rid of me? Would my dad let me live with him?

I spent the rest of the day thinking about what Sharon had said. I was thinking so hard I didn't even hear Ms. Maxwell when she asked me a question in social studies.

"Well, Tracy?"

I looked up, feeling silly. I knew we were studying something about Australia, but I wasn't sure what.

"Kangaroos," I said, taking a wild guess. The class laughed.

"I asked you to name the oceans surrounding Australia," she said. "Pay attention."

I tried, but I couldn't stop thinking about Walter. Did he really want to get rid of me?

That night, while Mom and I were getting dinner ready, I asked her if she wanted to get rid of Ronald.

"No, of course not." She stirred the soup, then looked at me thoughtfully. "What makes you ask?"

I didn't want to tell her about what Sharon had said. "Well, he's not very nice."

"It's hard for him living with two strangers, just like it's hard for you." She bent down and kissed my hair. "Don't worry. Nobody is getting rid of anybody around here."

The next day we had to hand in our continent books. Before I left for school, I looked at mine again. I was really proud of what a good job I had done. All my continents were neatly labeled and the oceans had neat blue waves in them.

When I left for school I was humming. I couldn't wait to tell Sharon that she was wrong about Walter wanting to get rid of me. When I got to Sharon's corner I looked down the street to see if she was coming.

I didn't see Micky until it was too late. Before I knew it, he'd knocked me down. Then he grabbed my booklet of the continents.

"Give me that back!" I screamed. "Or I'm going to tell on you!"

Micky just stood there, looking down at me with a big smile on his face.

"Any Stacy is an enemy of mine," he said. Then he ran off with my booklet.

"You come back here," I yelled. When I stood up, I saw my knee was bleeding a little. Boy, was I mad! My hands were scraped and my dress was torn.

After what had happened, I didn't feel so good. Besides, how could I go to school without my project? I knew my mom wasn't working, so I decided to turn around and go home.

"Tracy!" my mom said when I came through the back door into the kitchen. "What are you doing back here?"

"I fell off my bike and I feel sick." I tried not to start crying.

Mom washed my knee, and kissed it to make

it better. Even though I know that kissing cuts is for babies, I let her.

I pretended to be sick. Mom put me to bed and even put a TV set in my room. I didn't even really have to pretend I was sick. My stomach hurt and I felt awful all over.

I thought about Micky the whole day while I watched movies. Why did he say, "Any Stacy is an enemy of mine"? Maybe Ronald knew. And what about my booklet? Instead of thinking that I get good grades, Ms. Maxwell would think I didn't bother to hand in projects.

If I told on Micky, I'd be a tattletale. None of the other kids would talk to me. The whole thing made me so upset I couldn't eat dinner. Not even the strawberry tart Mom made for dessert.

"Aren't you feeling better, Tracy?" Mom asked when she saw I wasn't eating. "Strawberry is your favorite."

"I'm allergic to strawberries," Ronald said to her, pretending I didn't exist. "I told you before. Strawberries and peanuts."

"I didn't know, but I'll remember in the future," Mom promised.

Ronald pushed his strawberry tart across the table. "I know you're trying to poison me, but it won't work," he said, scowling.

"Don't talk that way to your stepmother," Walter said.

Ronald scowled at his father and stood up from the table.

"Ronald," I said, "do you know a guy named Micky Snipper?"

"Yeah, I know him," Ronald said, making a face. "He was in my grade last year, but he's so dumb he got left back."

I was surprised. That was about the longest thing Ronald ever said to me. "Did you guys have a fight?" I asked.

"Last year he tried to pick on me and Elliot, so we ganged up on him a few times." Ronald frowned at me. "Why do you want to know?"

I looked over at my mom to make sure she wasn't listening. Luckily, she was busy clearing the table. "He knocked me down today and stole my book of the continents," I whispered. I wasn't sure I should trust Ronald, but I knew if I told my mom, she'd call my teacher.

"So what?" Ronald said loudly.

"*Shh,*" I said, pointing at Mom. I didn't want her to hear. "Micky told me he hated all Stacys," I whispered.

He looked at me angrily. "So? You're not a Stacy."

"I don't want to be a Stacy. I just don't want Micky picking on me." I knew I should never have told Ronald.

Mom turned around. She must have heard

the whole thing. "Why didn't you tell me about this?" she asked sharply.

I stared down at my plate and didn't say anything. "I'm going to call your teacher," Mom said.

"No, don't," I pleaded. "I'll be a tattletale."

"Listen, Tracy," Mom said firmly, "I can't have people knocking you down and stealing your projects. I'll tell Ms. Maxwell what happened, and I promise she'll be discreet."

"What does 'discreet' mean?" I asked.

"It means that she'll keep Micky from hurting you without anyone knowing why she's doing it."

I didn't say anything, but I felt better. So much better I had two slices of strawberry tart—mine and Ronald's.

◆ Chapter 5 ◆

*T*he next day at school, Ms. Maxwell asked me for my continent project.

"I lost it, but I'll make it up," I said.

"You don't have to," Ms. Maxwell said. "I found it." She handed it to me. There was an A on the cover.

"I knew it was yours because of the little waves you put in the water. Somebody else handed it in," she said.

She raised her voice and looked out at the class. "And that somebody will have to stay after school this week and make it up."

Everyone was looking around the class to see who that somebody was. I looked hard at Micky. Soon everyone was looking at him. He glared at me.

I was glad he was going to be staying after school.

Most of all, I felt happy for myself. Mom made it work out just like she said it would.

Later in the day, we played kickball against the fourth-graders, and Micky was on my team. I tried not to look at him. When Ronald saw him, he said, "Hey, dummy, get any C's lately?" If it were anyone else, I would have felt bad.

Ronald was pitching. "Yo, dog face," he said when it was my turn to kick. "Scare any cats today?"

I made a face at him. He rolled the ball. I kicked it as hard as I could and got a triple. A girl in my class named Amy and a third-grader I didn't know were on second and third, so my kick got us two points.

"Capital, just capital," shouted Amy when she got to home base. Amy was always saying weird stuff like "capital" and "splendid" because her family had a British nanny.

"Even a girl can beat you," Micky yelled to Ronald. The next person up kicked the ball right to Ronald. But instead of throwing it to first base, Ronald threw the ball as hard as he could right at me. It hit me in the head, and I fell down. All the kids crowded around me. After seeing that I was okay, Mr. Boggs yelled at Ronald.

"I didn't mean to hurt her, Mr. Boggs," Ronald said. "I just wanted to make an out."

Mr. Boggs made him apologize, anyway. "I'm sorry, Tracy," Ronald said. He was smiling. I never saw a less sorry person in my life.

I got up and glared at Ronald. "You did that on purpose, and you know it," I said.

"Now, now, Tracy," Mr. Boggs said, "accidents happen." He made us shake hands. Then he asked if I was sure that I was okay.

"I'm fine. He didn't hurt me at all. Not a single little bit," I yelled at Ronald.

Mr. Boggs looked at my head. "Well, there's no swelling," he said with a frown. "Still, I don't think you should be alone at home. Is your mom there?"

I looked down at my feet. All this attention was beginning to make me feel silly. "She's working today," I mumbled.

"Why doesn't Tracy come home with me Mr. Boggs?" Sharon said. "I live right nearby and my mom'll be home at four."

"Good idea," Mr. Boggs said. I was so happy Sharon had invited me to her house I could have kissed Ronald.

After school, I got my bike and waited for Sharon. She came out with a group of girls. "Leslie, Amy and Linda are coming over, too," Sharon said, pointing to the three girls. "We're going to do each other's hair. Linda is a great

hairdresser," Sharon said. She patted Linda's arm.

Linda looked down at the ground and blushed. She was the shiest girl in class, but she was so nice that everyone liked her. "That's because I do my mother's hair," she whispered.

"Linda's mother is divorced, too," said Sharon.

"Linda has had three stepdads," Amy said.

"Wow," I said. "Do you have stepbrothers and sisters?"

"So far, I've had seven stepbrothers and three stepsisters," Linda said.

Seven Ronalds. I would die.

Sharon's house was only a few blocks away from school. After stopping off in the kitchen for cookies, we all trooped upstairs to her room.

Sharon pulled out an old magazine. It said *Movie Star Hairstyles* on the cover.

"My babysitter gave it to me. I like this one the best." Sharon pointed to a picture of a neat-looking girl wearing a bun. "It's called a twister."

Linda studied the picture. "Let's try it."

"Splendid idea," said Amy.

Leslie, Amy and I ate cookies while Linda worked on Sharon. We were all talking about Ronald. Did he try to hit me on purpose or not? Everybody thought so but Linda.

"You should give him the benefit of the

doubt," Linda said. How could a person who had seven stepbrothers be so nice?

A few minutes later Linda turned Sharon around. "What do you think?"

I thought it looked awful, but didn't want to say so. Luckily we heard a car door slam out in the driveway. The noise saved me from having to answer.

"That's my mom," Sharon said. We ran downstairs to meet her.

Sharon's mother came in with a little girl. "Hi, brat. Hi, Mom," Sharon said. "How do you like my hair?"

"It's very different, darling," Sharon's mother said, bending down to kiss her. She was carrying the ugliest lamp I'd ever seen. Sharon introduced me to her mother and little half-sister, Debbie.

"Quite a find, isn't it?" Sharon's mother said, pointing to her lamp.

"It's . . . uh, very different," I said.

Pretty soon it was time for me to go home. "So long, Sharon," I said.

" 'Bye, Tracy. Why don't you come over tomorrow after school?"

"You mean it?" I asked.

Sharon nodded. Leslie didn't look too happy, but I was thrilled. I left Sharon's feeling happy. Finally, I'd made some friends.

I was in such a good mood that I even

forgot to tell Mom that Ronald hit me in the head with a volleyball.

Soon Sharon and I were eating lunch together every day. Leslie didn't like our friendship, though. Not one little bit. First she tried to ignore me. Then she started talking about me behind my back. When I'd come into a room, there would be a little silence. Or she'd whisper something to Amy or Linda right in front of me.

At first, I tried not to let it bother me. But it did. Finally, one day at lunch I said something.

"How come you're always whispering?" I asked her.

"Because I don't want you to hear things," said Leslie. She stood up and put her hands on her hips. "You think you can come to Greatdale and change everything. Well, you can't."

"Yeah," said Amy. She stood up with her hands on her hips just like Leslie. She was such a copycat.

Linda stared down at her half-eaten sandwich. I could tell she felt bad. Leslie grabbed her tray.

"We're leaving," she said to Sharon. "And I suggest that you drop your little friend here."

Little friend, I thought. I wanted to punch her right in the nose.

"Capital idea," said Amy.

Sharon stood up, too. "And if I don't?" she asked.

"Then we can't be friends anymore," said Leslie.

"I like Tracy," Sharon said.

I guess that was that, because Amy picked up her tray, and she and Leslie marched across the room.

"Come on, Linda," Leslie called.

Linda didn't move. She just sat there, staring down at her tray.

I looked at Sharon. She looked like she was going to cry.

"I'm sorry, Sharon," I told her. "It was all my fault."

"No, it wasn't," Sharon said bravely. "I don't care about them, anyway." I knew she was lying. Still, I felt pretty good that she had stuck up for me.

Leslie didn't speak to Sharon or me for the rest of the day. Neither did Amy.

I thought that Sharon and Leslie would make up in a couple of days. But they didn't. I kept waiting for Sharon to bring it up.

Finally, on Halloween, I asked her about it. "Do you want to ask Leslie to come trick-or-treating with us?"

Sharon sighed. "You know she won't be friends with me if you and I are friends."

"Oh," I said quietly. I looked down at the ground. "Do you, um, want to drop me?" I said in a little voice. It was a tough question to ask.

"No, I don't." Sharon tossed her head like she always does when she's mad. "No one can tell me what to do." She smiled. "Besides, I really like you."

I put out my hand. "Best friends?" I said.

"Yeah," Sharon said. We shook on it.

After school, Sharon and I changed into our costumes. I was dressed as Cinderella, and she was going as Wonder Woman.

As soon as we finished dressing, we ran out to go trick-or-treating. We had only gone about two blocks when . . . splat. I felt something hit my head. It cracked and dripped down through my hair. Splat. Another one. Splat. Splat.

"Eggs," Sharon yelled. We ran and ducked behind a hedge.

"Can you see them?" Sharon whispered. She wiped the egg off her face with her sleeve. Her Wonder Woman makeup smeared all over her face.

I peered through the hedge. I couldn't see anyone in front of us. Down the street some girls were trick-or-treating.

"I think they're gone," I said to Sharon. I stood up. An egg hit me in the chest.

I ducked back down. "Wrong," Sharon laughed. She didn't seem to mind the fact that her whole costume was getting ruined.

"We can't stay here forever," I told her. "Let's make a run for it." Sharon and I grabbed hands, and together we started running down the street. An egg hit me in the back.

"Faster," I yelled. We ran past the three girls dressed as bears.

"Let's get them," I heard one of the girls shout. I turned around. The three girls were throwing eggs at the boys. The boys were outnumbered. They ran down the street.

"Chicken," Sharon yelled after them. She turned to the girls. "Good going," she said.

The girls took off their bear masks. It was Leslie, Amy, and Linda. "We're the three bears," Linda said, giggling.

"You are three great bears," Sharon said.

Leslie looked at Sharon and started to laugh. "You should see yourself."

I looked at Sharon, too. Her makeup was half-off, and she had egg in her hair and face. "You do look pretty funny," I said, cracking up.

"You think I look funny?" Sharon asked. "You should see how you look." She turned to the girls. "Tracy and I have to go change. Do you want to come over?"

"Nah, we're going to finish trick-or-treating," Leslie said. "Maybe tomorrow?"

Leslie and Sharon smiled at each other. They were friends again. I felt a pang in my stomach. Could Sharon be friends with both me and Leslie?

Chapter 6

I was a little late for school the next day. When I got to my desk, Sharon and Leslie were talking and giggling.

I sat down. "Hi, guys," I said.

Sharon grinned at me. "Hi," she said.

Leslie didn't smile. She just nodded. I figured no matter what I did, she was never going to like me.

At lunch I sat by myself. I wasn't hungry. I took out a book and started reading, but I couldn't get into it. I kept reading the same sentence over and over.

Someone tapped my arm. I looked up.

"There you are," Sharon said. "I've been looking all over for you." She sat down next to me.

"Hi," I said. I looked back down at my book. "Sure you don't want to eat with Leslie?"

"Are we best friends or aren't we?" Sharon said. She smiled at me.

Suddenly I was starving. "We sure are," I said, taking a big bite out of my sandwich. "We sure are."

Greatdale was freezing already, and it wasn't even Thanksgiving yet. Not that I was looking forward to it. Grandma Connie was coming for dinner.

On Thanksgiving morning, it snowed. Walter took Ronald to the Inn. I stayed home to help Mom make the Thanksgiving bird.

I was glad it was just going to be the two of us. It sounds funny because I lived with Mom, but sometimes I really missed her. When we lived alone in Brooklyn we used to hang around the house together and laugh. Now, whenever I was home, Walter or Ronald were around, too. It just wasn't the same.

Instead of a turkey, Mom was making wild pheasant. She cooked it with bacon and apples, and made side dishes of snail stuffing, cranberry relish, roasted artichoke, and carrot salad.

Dinner was great. Mom's been trying her recipes out on me since I was little, so I love weird food. She always brags about what grown-up taste I have in foods.

Walter even had thirds. He didn't have grown-up taste like me, though. He was just a pig.

Ronald just picked at his plate. Grandma Connie hardly ate a thing.

"Try the stuffing," Mom said.

She took a taste and made a face like she just bit into a lemon. "Mmm. What's in it?" she asked.

"Bread, onion, butter, spices and snails."

Grandma Connie put her hand over her mouth. "My, my, how original," she said.

Then Ronald started making a grating sound in his throat. "Eh, eh, eh."

I jumped out of my seat. I remembered when he threw up at the barbecue.

"Snails!" he cried, clutching his throat. "That's the most disgusting thing I've ever heard."

"Try them," Mom said. "They're very tasty."

"I'm not eating any snails," Ronald yelled.

"I spent all day making this food, and I want you to try it," Mom said to Ronald.

"You can't tell me what to do. I already have a mother," Ronald shouted.

"Yeah? Where is she?" I asked. "I've been living here since August and I haven't seen or heard from her once!"

Ronald clenched his fists and turned purple. I stared at him. I had never seen a human being turn that color before.

"Ahhh!" he screamed. Then he leaped up out of his chair and ran toward me. Luckily I'm fast. I ducked under the table. He grabbed my chair and hurled it out of the way.

"I'm going to kill you!" Ronald screamed.

Walter got up and ran over to him. He picked him up and carried him out of the room.

A few minutes later Walter came back to the table. The four of us finished our meal in silence. I could hear the sound of Ronald sobbing upstairs.

Finally, Grandma Connie spoke to my mother. "I'm not one to butt in—" she started to say.

Mom cut her off. "Then don't," she said firmly.

Grandma Connie looked shocked. "I can see when I'm not wanted," she said to Walter. She picked up her coat and walked out of the house.

Mom put her head in her hands. "I'm sorry," she said to Walter.

Walter went over and put his arm around her shoulder. "It's hard," he said. Mom looked up at him and smiled. He bent down and kissed her head.

"I'll go talk to Ronald," he said.

When he went upstairs, Mom explained that Ronald's mother had walked out on him and Walter when Ronald was still a baby.

He only talked to her a couple of times a year.

"Ronald feels very bad about it," Mom said, "so you shouldn't tease him."

Later, I went upstairs and knocked on Ronald's door.

"Who is it?" he said through the door.

"It's me! Tracy!" I yelled. "Please, Ronald, let me in." I tried the door, but I couldn't open it. "I'm sorry," I called.

He didn't say anything. "Can you hear me?" I asked.

"Go away," he said.

I went to talk to Mom, but she was in her room with the door closed. She didn't want to talk to me, either.

I decided to call Dad. "Happy Thanksgiving, Daddy."

"Happy Thanksgiving, pumpkin," he said.

"You're never going to lose touch with me, will you?"

"Not in a million, billion years."

I told my daddy what happened at dinner. "And now Ronald really hates me."

"You know, pumpkin, there's an old saying: you can catch more flies with honey than you can with vinegar. That means that if you want people to like you, you have to be nice to them. Think about it."

I thought about it.

Chapter 7

*R*onald didn't speak to me for a week. After that he seemed to forgive me, but he didn't forget. A couple of weeks later, he accidentally-on-purpose spilled milk on my skirt.

I was sitting with Sharon, Leslie, Amy and Linda. We were all getting along, eating lunch and talking. Until Ronald ran by. He reached out and knocked the milk off my tray. The carton flew into my lap and spilled all over my new skirt.

"I'm so sorry," Ronald said in this really fake voice.

I didn't believe him, so I punched him in the stomach.

"What's going on here?" Mr. Boggs shouted. "What are you doing, Tracy?"

Ronald told him about how I punched him. But before I could explain why, Mr. Boggs was yelling at me.

"Don't ever let me catch you hitting your stepbrother again! Understand?"

I gulped back my tears. It wasn't fair. I was the one covered in milk. Besides, I didn't hit him very hard.

I decided to get even with Ronald if it was the last thing I did. Every day Sharon and I went to her house to talk about it. Sharon had the first idea.

"Let's put a bat in his room," she said.

"Yuck," I said, making a face. "Besides, where are we going to get a bat?"

"In a cave. Remember that television show we saw about bats?"

I shook my head. "I don't know, Sharon. It's a mean thing to do to a little bat."

"You're probably right," Sharon said.

Then I had a great idea. I told Sharon about it, and she agreed it would work. So one morning when Mom wasn't looking, I replaced the roast beef in Ronald's sandwich with mud. I covered the mud with lettuce, tomato and Russian dressing. At lunch, Sharon and I grabbed seats right across from Ronald. We didn't want to miss the show.

Ronald bit into his sandwich without looking. Then he made this horrible face and spat the whole thing out onto the table. I couldn't stop laughing.

Mr. Boggs saw what happened. He sent Ronald to the boys' room to rinse out his mouth. Then he turned to me.

"What are you laughing about, Tracy?" he asked.

"Nothing." I was laughing so hard I could barely speak. Mr. Boggs made me take the sandwich to the principal's office. I got a lecture and a discipline slip.

I wasn't laughing when I told Mom she had to sign my slip. She was mad, but not half as mad as Walter.

He gave me a lecture, too—a long one. "We're a family now, Tracy, and you have to make more of an effort to get along with Ronald."

He made it sound like the whole thing was my fault. "You didn't yell at Ronald when he spilled milk on my skirt," I said.

"That was an accident," Ronald said hotly.

"Sure," I said.

Then Walter made me apologize to Ronald.

"I'm sorry for putting mud in your sandwich, Ronald," I said. But when I remembered how funny he had looked, I started to laugh again.

"No, you're not," he grumbled. He took a step forward like he was going to hit me.

"Yes, I am." I giggled. "Really sorry."

"See, Dad," Ronald said. "She's not sorry at all."

"That's it!" Walter said. "Go to your room, Tracy."

I had to eat dinner there all by myself. And no television for a week. I promised myself again that I'd get even with Ronald if it was the last thing I did.

Christmas vacation was even better than I thought it would be. My dad took me skiing, and I took a lesson every day. Then, at the end of the week, Dad took me all the way up to the top of the mountain. It was great. I wished I could ski forever.

The night before I was supposed to go home, Mom called. She and Dad had a long talk. After they hung up, Dad sat me down. "Mom tells me that you and Walter don't get along."

"I don't get along with Ronald, either."

I could see that Dad was trying not to smile. "Let's talk about Walter for now."

I looked down at the floor. "I hate him."

Dad lifted my chin up so I was looking at him. "Why?" he asked softly.

I sighed. "Because he's fat and ugly."

Dad laughed. Then he turned serious. "You

know," he said, "you can love me and still like Walter. Even love him."

"Yeah?" I said, looking up. I never thought of that.

"No matter how well you and Walter get along, you'll always be my special girl." Dad pulled me into his arms, and gave me a big hug.

I smiled up at him. "And you'll always be my special dad," I said.

◆ Chapter 8 ◆

I decided that my resolution for the new year would be to get along better with Walter. I tried really hard. But it's hard to get along with someone who won't believe you're telling the truth.

About a month after I got home, I noticed Ronald and Walter were playing checkers with my checker set. "Who gave you permission to play with my stuff?" I asked Ronald.

"Listen, dog breath, these checkers happen to belong to me," Ronald said.

I walked into the den to get a better look. "They do not, and for your information, my name isn't dog breath," I yelled.

Walter cleared his throat. "Er . . . do these checkers belong to Tracy, Ronald?" he asked.

Ronald looked him right in the eye. "No, Dad. They're mine."

"If you tell me they're yours, son, I believe you," Walter said. I turned and ran out of the room. What about me? Why wouldn't Walter believe me? I was as good as Ronald.

I was angry. I knew Ronald stole my checkers. That was the final straw.

The next morning, I took his math homework out of his textbook and tore it up. I figured he'd think it fell out of his book on his way to school. But things didn't work out that way.

I was just finishing my breakfast when Ronald started flipping through his notebook. "I can't find my homework," he announced.

Walter looked up from his paper. "Look in your room," he said.

Ronald tore out of the kitchen. In a few minutes I heard him yell from upstairs. "I can't find it!" He ran back into the kitchen. I started to giggle nervously.

"What do you know about this, young lady?" Mom asked. She must have seen me laugh.

"Nothing," I said, giggling.

"Don't lie to me, Tracy," Mom said. "I can see you know something."

Then I got scared. I realized throwing out Ronald's homework was a pretty big offense. "I tore it up," I whispered.

"You *what*?" Walter yelled.

"I tore it up." I pointed to the garbage bag in the kitchen. Ronald ran over to it and picked out a handful of ripped-up papers.

"I can't hand this in," Ronald yelled. He made a ball out of his homework and threw it at me. It missed.

"I'll write you a note," Walter said.

"As for you, young lady," Mom said, "no going to Sharon's after school for the next week and no television."

"How come he can steal my checkers and nothing happens to him?" I yelled.

"I told you I didn't take your cruddy checkers," Ronald yelled back.

I stuck my tongue out at him.

Walter looked at me angrily. "Stop it, Tracy. You're lucky the punishment isn't harsher."

"You're all mean to me," I screamed as I ran out of the house. I got on my bike and rode to school.

At least school was interesting. In science, Ms. Maxwell broke our class into groups. Sharon and Leslie were in my group, along with two boys I didn't know very well, Andrew and Robbie. Each group had to do a report on some part of the solar system. My group was studying Jupiter.

"You can do either an oral or a written report," Ms. Maxwell said.

"Only an idiot would do a written report if he could get away with an oral one," Andrew whispered.

The first day we got together, my whole group went to the library. We took out a bunch of books on Jupiter. Then everyone came to my house.

At first, no one had any ideas. We sat in the basement eating Mom's brownies and looking through the library books. Finally, Robbie looked up from his book. "Let's do life on Jupiter."

Andrew pushed up his glasses. "That would make a pretty short report," he said, "since there isn't any."

"That's why it's such a good idea," Robbie said eagerly.

"Ms. Maxwell is nice, but there's no way she'd let us get away with that," said Leslie.

"Why don't we each study something about Jupiter and do an oral report on it?" said Robbie.

Sharon gave a big yawn. "Boring!" she said. "The class would be asleep in five minutes."

Robbie looked hurt. "Let's see you come up with some ideas," he said.

"You know," I said, smiling at Robbie, "I like Robbie's first idea. Let's do a report on what our life would be like if we lived on Jupiter."

Andrew screwed up his face like he was really thinking. "I don't know," he said.

"That's a great idea," Sharon said excitedly. "But let's do it in a new way."

"How about a television show?" said Leslie.

"I've got it!" I said, jumping up and down. "Let's do it like a news show. I could be the anchor. I could do an introduction, then say, 'Here's Leslie, live, to talk about the weather on Jupiter's red spot.'"

Everyone loved the idea. We decided that we'd make a big model of a television for us to sit behind. We'd each come up with a topic.

Andrew and Robbie would make the model television. Leslie, Sharon and I would write the news stories. We'd get together and work at least once a week.

After the meeting, I went upstairs to see Mom. She was hemming a skirt. "Tracy, you have to get along better with Walter and Ronald. Not only for their sake, but for yours, too. . . ."

Yap, yap, yap, I thought as she droned on. I was hardly listening. Watching her sew, I had a wonderful idea for a new trick to play on Ronald. I had the perfect day for it, too. Easter Assembly.

A few weeks later, I took Ronald's good pants off the ironing board. Using Mom's tiny nail clippers, I cut out most of the seam along the seat. Because I didn't remove it all, the pants still looked okay.

I knew that he'd be wearing them the next day for assembly. Ronald's class was reciting a poem they wrote.

As soon as I got to school, I told Sharon what I'd done. "It would be great if he splits them right in the middle of assembly," Sharon whispered to me in math class.

"That's the idea," I whispered back.

"Sharon, Tracy, if you don't stop whispering, I'm going to have to separate you." Ms. Maxwell said, looking at us sternly. "And if you don't pay attention, you'll never learn the nine table. Then where would you be?"

I'd be a lot happier, but I didn't tell Ms. Maxwell that.

Assembly wasn't until the end of the day. Ronald's class went first. It seemed like their poem went on forever. Ronald had the last two lines. "Let's forgive and forget. I want to, you bet." The audience applauded.

"They're not applauding the poem," I whispered to Sharon. "Everyone's just glad that it's over."

Ronald's class bowed and walked off. As Ronald turned, I saw his pants had split right in two. The audience began to laugh. I was giggling so hard by now that Ms. Maxwell had to send me into the hallway to calm down.

That afternoon, my group was coming over for its final meeting. Andrew and Robbie had made a beautiful television. It had little knobs on the bottom and everything. We all had our speeches worked out. I was keeping the model television in my basement. Mom promised she'd drive me to school in the morning.

After my study group left, Ronald couldn't find his notebook. Naturally, he blamed me. I was downstairs in the basement practicing my speech.

"Give me my notebook, Tracy," he shouted to me.

I pretended not to hear him. In a minute I could hear him coming down the stairs. He came over to me with his hand out. "I said, give me my notebook," he said again.

"I don't have your stupid notebook," I said, backing away.

"I know you stole it, and I'm sick of your dumb tricks."

I gave him a big smile. "My tricks sure made a fool out of you."

"What do you mean, dog face?" Ronald grabbed my arm. "Tell me or I'll break your arm."

"Let go." I struggled to get away, but Ronald held my arm tightly. "Mom!"

"Tell me."

"You think you're so smart," I yelled. "Well,

who do you think split your pants, smarty? Me."

Ronald was so surprised he let go of my arm. "You did not," he said.

"I did so," I said, rubbing my arm. "I cut out the seam with Mom's little clippers." I laughed. "Boy, did you look funny."

"Let's see if you find this funny." Ronald kicked a hole through my television. Before I could stop him, he had completely kicked it apart.

Ronald and I were crying and screaming by the time Mom and Walter got downstairs. I've never seen Mom so angry. Or Walter.

"No television for a whole month. Both of you." Walter stormed back upstairs.

Mom just shook her head. "I'm very disappointed in you, Tracy. And you, too, Ronald." Then she followed Walter back upstairs.

I felt awful about what had happened. And what was my study group going to say? Mom wasn't the only one who was going to be disappointed, that's for sure.

Chapter 9

*T*hat afternoon, I tried to rebuild the television set but couldn't get it back together. I started to cry. My whole group was going to hate me.

As soon as dinner was over, I called Dad. He couldn't help me, either. "Actions have consequences, Tracy. You embarrassed Ronald, and he struck back."

"But what about my group?"

"They're not going to be happy, but from what you told me, the television was only a prop."

"But Andrew and Robbie worked so hard." I started crying again.

"I wish I could come over and help you," Dad said. "But I'm too far away. Why don't you call your friend Sharon and see if she can come over?"

Dad always had good ideas. I hung up the phone and called Sharon, but she couldn't come either. "Mom won't let me come out. I'm being punished for hitting the brat," she said.

A few minutes later the doorbell rang. Leslie was standing on the front steps.

"What are you doing here?" I asked her.

"Sharon called me," she said.

Leslie tried to get our model back together, but she couldn't do it, either. "I give up," she said finally. "Let's make another one."

Together we cut a frame out of cardboard, and covered the back in clear cellophane. I drew in the knobs. Our model television didn't look great, but it would have to do.

"Thank you, Leslie," I said when she was leaving. "I couldn't have done it without you."

"Hey"—she shrugged her shoulders—"what are friends for?"

I dreaded going to school the next day. I knew I had to face Robbie and Andrew.

"I can't believe you let this happen," Robbie said. He sounded pretty angry.

"It looks awful," Andrew said, looking at the television Leslie and I had made.

"What's important is the whole report, not

just the television," said Leslie. She smiled at me. I was really glad she was on my side.

"That's what you say," said Robbie.

"Listen, everyone," I said. "I'll tell Ms. Maxwell what happened and explain how it was all my fault."

"I don't think that will help," Robbie said, turning away from me. I felt bad. I knew he wanted to show the thing to his dad. Andrew didn't say anything. He just played with his glasses and looked sad.

Our group was the last to speak. I thought we did the best job. Ms. Maxwell seemed to like it, too. She told us that our report was factual and that we presented it with a lot of style.

I waited after school to talk to her. I told her everything, even how I split Ronald's pants. I ended by saying, "Please don't take it out on the group, Ms. Maxwell. If you want to give anyone a low grade, give it to me."

"It was very brave of you to tell me, Tracy," she said, "and I'll take this conversation under advisement."

"What does that mean?" I asked.

"That means that I'll consider everything you said before making up my mind."

Sharon and Leslie were waiting for me outside school. I told them what Ms. Maxwell said.

"Don't worry, Tracy," said Leslie, "Our group was the best. Besides, like your dad said, the television was only a prop."

"Sticking up for Tracy, I see," Sharon said. She didn't say it very nicely.

"Like you never make a mistake," Leslie snapped back at her.

Sharon and Leslie glared at each other. They didn't say anything for the longest time. Finally I spoke up. "Don't be mad at each other," I pleaded. "The whole thing was really my fault." Sharon looked at Leslie. Then she smiled.

"I know. I'm sorry," she said.

"Me, too," said Leslie. The three of us walked over to our bikes. I hoped we would all be friends now.

Ms. Maxwell gave everyone in our group an A. She can take my work under advisement anytime she wants. I was glad it was our last project for the year, though. I was ready for summer.

Both Ronald and I were going away. I was going to Maine to be with Dad, and Ronald was going to camp in New Hampshire. I'll bet Mom and Walter were glad to be rid of us.

They'd been fighting a lot lately, and it was mostly about us. Walter said Mom was spoiling me and that I had no manners. Mom said Walter was spoiling Ronald.

One Friday, Walter and Mom had a big fight. It happened because Walter and Ronald came home late from a baseball game. Mom and I were waiting for them so we could all have dinner together.

"None for us," Walter said when they got home. "We ate on the way home."

Mom looked upset. "Why did you do that?" she asked. "Tracy and I were keeping dinner."

"I wanted some peace and quiet," Walter said.

Mom untied her apron and threw it at Walter. "It will be nice and quiet when I'm not speaking to you," she yelled. A minute later, I heard her slam the bedroom door.

Walter started cleaning the kitchen. I took a plate of food and went into the den to watch television. Ronald was watching an adventure movie.

I picked up the remote control. "I want to watch *The Sound of Music*," I said. Ronald grabbed the remote out of my hands.

"Too bad, dog face," he said. I tried to get the remote back, but Ronald bashed me with it.

"Mom! Ronald hit me," I yelled.

"She started it."

Walter ran into the den and grabbed Ronald's arm. Mom was right behind him. "I've had enough," Walter said. "I can't stand all this bickering. Tonight," he said, looking at Ronald, "you can watch whatever you want, because tonight we're sleeping at the Inn."

"Oh, boy!" Ronald said. He started jumping up and down.

"You're leaving?" Mom cried.

"I can't take it anymore, Susan. I need some time off."

They left. Mom just stood there and cried. I didn't know what to do.

Walter and Ronald stayed away all weekend. I tried to enjoy being alone with Mom, but all she did was cry.

Monday morning, Ronald and Walter still weren't home. I couldn't wait for school to end on Monday afternoon. The minute the bell rang, I jumped on my bike. I wanted to see if Walter and Ronald were back.

On the way home, I passed a field where flowers were growing wild. I decided to stop and pick some for Mom. I was putting the flowers in my bicycle basket when Micky Snipper pulled up on his bike next to me.

"Now I've got you, Tracy Stacy," he said. He put his hands on my handlebars. I was too angry to be scared.

"My name is Crane," I said loudly. I tried to pull the bike away from him, but he was too strong. "Let go of my bike," I shouted.

Micky lifted it up and held it over his head.

He gave me a nasty smile. "You want it, get it," he taunted.

"Give it to me!" I yelled. I grabbed Micky's arm and tried to pull it down, but I couldn't. "Give it back!"

I heard a branch snap behind me. I looked around. Ronald and Elliot were standing there.

"Give my sister her bike back," Ronald said. The boys came forward. Micky dropped the bike and ran.

"Look at him go," Ronald said.

"Fatter than a speeding bullet," said Elliot. The boys laughed and slapped hands.

I picked my bike up off the ground. It was fine and I felt like a fool. "I can take care of myself." I said. "And I'm not your sister, and I hate your guts."

"Don't thank me for anything," Ronald said. "I only saved your life."

I glared at him. He was right, but I didn't care. I got back on my bike.

Elliot rubbed his hands together. "Now that Micky's gone, we can get her ourselves," he said in a funny, high-pitched voice.

The boys started toward me. I stuck my tongue out at them. Then I rode off at top speed. I could hear them laughing behind me.

Chapter 10

When I got home, I thought about how lucky I was. If Ronald hadn't saved me, Micky might have ruined my bike.

I wanted to thank him. But he wouldn't talk to me. I tried to ask Mom about it. But when I knocked on her door, Walter opened it. I didn't want to talk to Walter about Ronald. I wasn't even sure he and Mom had made up.

"Yes, Tracy," Walter said.

"Are you back for good?" I asked him.

He didn't say anything. I felt my cheeks getting red. I didn't mean for it to come out that way, but there was no way I could take it back now. I turned and ran into my room.

Dinner was strange. Everyone was quiet and

really polite. I tried to talk, but no one would talk back. It seemed like everyone was mad at me.

After dinner I called Dad. I told him everything. How Ronald and I had fought. How it was causing trouble between Walter and Mom. How Ronald saved me this afternoon. How I was mean to him. How I wanted to make up but didn't know how.

Dad didn't say a word the whole time I was talking. When I finished, he said, "When you want to be friends with other people, you're nice to them, right?"

I thought for a minute. "Yeah," I said slowly.

"You talk with them. You compliment them. If you hurt their feelings, you apologize."

I knew he was right. I sighed. "So, if you want to be friends with Ronald, you'll have to act like a friend. Friends don't tell their friends they hate their guts."

I felt bad. "I know," I said slowly. "But, Dad, he's been mean to me, too. Almost all the time."

"He wasn't today," Dad said. "Was he?"

Dad was right. Ronald had been nice to me and I blew it.

"It took a long time for you and Ronald to get so angry at each other," Dad said. "It made a pattern, and it will take awhile for you to change that pattern. But when you do, it'll be worth it."

"Thanks, Dad," I said. After I hung up the phone, I thought a lot about what my dad had said.

Later that night I knocked on Ronald's door. "Thank you for saving me from Micky," I yelled through the door. "I don't hate you. And I'm sorry I said you weren't my brother."

The next day at breakfast, I said good morning to Ronald. He didn't answer. "I'm glad school is almost over, aren't you?" I asked him.

He didn't even look up. "Don't bother me," he said. "I'm doing my homework."

I tried hard to be nice to Ronald. Once I even took out the garbage for him. At first he ignored me.

But after a few days of being nice to Ronald, he began to warm up.

"I wish I could do wheelies as good as you," I said. I was standing in front of the house watching Ronald practice tricks on his skateboard.

"Well, dream on, dog face," Ronald said. But he looked pleased.

Later that night we were watching television. "That's a nice sweater," I said when the commercial came on.

"Yeah, well try not to unravel it," Ronald said.

"I'll try," I said. Then I laughed. Ronald laughed, too. You know, being nice is a lot easier than being mean.

A few minutes later, we heard screaming coming from the bedroom. Walter and Mom were having a huge fight. Even though Ronald and I were watching television in the den, we could hear every word perfectly. Then I heard the sound of something breaking. Finally, a door slammed, really loud.

Ronald and I looked at each other. "Wow," Ronald said. "That was a big one."

"Yeah," I agreed. I had a knot in my stomach. "You think Mom and Walter will get divorced?"

"Maybe." Ronald started wiggling his foot like he does when he gets nervous.

I took a deep breath. "If they do, then Mom and I will have to move. I can't change schools again," I blurted out. I got up and started pacing around the den.

Ronald nodded. His foot was going a mile a minute.

"Think Walter will marry someone else?" I asked.

"He might. I hope it's not Mrs. Taft. She's always pinching my cheek and telling me how cute I am." He smiled shyly at me. "Besides, I think I might be getting used to you."

I grinned back at him. "What we need is a

plan," I said. I stared at the television set. I wasn't watching the show, though. I was thinking about Walter and Mom.

Suddenly I had a brainstorm. "Listen, Ronald," I said excitedly. "Let's get them to take us to a romantic movie."

"Forget it," Ronald said, shaking his head.

"No. It's a good idea. They'll get all mushy and they'll hold hands and hug and kiss. Like this." I started toward him making little kissing sounds.

"Get away from me," Ronald said, jumping out of his chair.

"Trust me," I said.

Mom and Walter couldn't believe that Ronald and I wanted to see *Falling In Love*.

The movie was boring. But Mom loved it. When she and Walter left the theater they were holding hands. Afterward, we all went to the sweet shop for sodas. Ronald and I looked at comics. Walter and Mom looked at each other.

"You did good," Ronald said, pointing with his head to Mom and Walter.

"*We* did good." I smiled.

"Friends." He looked like he meant it.

"Friends," I said. We shook hands.

Walter bought each of us a comic. Dad was right about my being friends with Walter. It didn't take anything away from him for Wal-

ter and me to be friends. Dad will always be my dad no matter who I'm friends with.

"Thanks, Walter," I said, smiling.

The next day was the last day of school. When it was over, I waited outside for Sharon, Leslie, Amy and Linda. We were going shopping.

They came toward me, laughing and singing. I waved to them.

"No more pencils, no more books, no more teacher's dirty looks," they sang.

I joined in, wheeling my bike alongside them. Third grade was finally over. And it really wasn't so bad. I learned multiplication, made a few friends and got used to my new family.

I'm even looking forward to next year. I have some great new ideas for tricks to play. Ronald does, too. Only from now on we're playing tricks *together*—on Micky Snipper!

Don't miss these other great paperbacks about kids who really know how to *Make the Grade!*